BY
THALIA KALKIPSAKIS

ILLUSTRATIONS BY
ASH OSWALD

FEIWEL AND FRIENDS
New York

J
Kal

A Feiwel and Friends Book
An Imprint of Macmillan

Library of Congress Cataloging-in-Publication Data
Available

ISBN: 978-0-312-34643-0

First published in Australia by E2, an imprint of Hardie
Grant Egmont. Illustration and design by
Ash Oswald.

First published in the United States by Feiwel and
Friends, an imprint of Macmillan

Feiwel and Friends logo designed by Filomena Tuosto

First U.S. Edition: 2007

10 9 8 7 6 5 4 3

www.feiwelandfriends.com

GO TO
WWW.MYGOGIRLSERIES.COM
FOR **FREE** GO GIRL! DOWNLOADS,
QUIZZES, READING CLUB GUIDES,
AND LOTS MORE GO GIRL! FUN.

Get to know the girls of

COMING SOON

CHAPTER
*ONE

My big sister Hannah hates me and I know why. It's because I was born after her.

When Hannah was three, I was born. Everyone said I was *sooooooo cute!* Mom says they stopped saying Hannah was cute, so she threw all my baby clothes down the toilet.

I look younger than I really am. I'm nine years old, but sometimes people think

I look six or seven.

Hannah calls me a baby doll, but she doesn't mean it in a nice way. She says I should try to look my age, but it's not my fault! I can't change how I look.

But now, it's even worse than ever. Hannah cut off my hair and Mom went crazy on her. Then Hannah stopped talking to me.

Strange, isn't it? Hannah cut off my hair and got into trouble, and she blames me for it!

She must really hate me, that girl. Let me explain.

We were watching TV and a show came on about hair. It said that a haircut can change the way you look. It can make you look older or younger.

Hannah said, "Maybe if we cut your hair, people wouldn't think you're so cute anymore!"

"Yeah," I said, not really listening.

Hannah turned off the TV. "Aren't you sick of people saying how cute you look?" she asked.

"Yeah," I said again, but now I *was* listening.

"So why don't we cut your hair short, so you look your age?" Hannah said.

I wasn't sure. It sounded exciting, cutting my hair. I liked the idea of doing something different and looking older. But it's a big

Short hair could make me look older.

thing to cut off all your hair. And I've had long hair all my life.

"But what would Mom say?" I said.

"Mom!" Hannah rolled her eyes. Her hair is dark and shoulder length. It kinks up around her ears.

"Why do you always worry what Mom

thinks? It's not Mom's hair, " she said.

She had a point. It wasn't Mom's hair, it was *my* hair.

"Come on, let's do it." Hannah's eyes looked bright with excitement.

It was exciting to do something like this together, just her and me. It felt a bit like the stories you read of sisters going shopping and trying on clothes together. It felt good—like Hannah liked me.

It also seemed a little naughty to do something without Mom knowing.

"OK," I said. "Let's do it."

Hannah smiled.

I bet my eyes looked as bright and excited as Hannah's.

CHAPTER TWO

I'll always remember the sound of the scissors cutting through my hair.

It was a kind of a crunching sound. You'd probably expect a *snip snip* kind of sound. But there was so much hair bunched together that the scissors made a sliding, crunching sound as Hannah cut.

My hair was tied in two pigtails. Hannah said she would cut off each pigtail, and then clean up my hair after that.

When she had cut off the first pigtail, Hannah held up the hair for me to see.

"Say good-bye to your hair, Cassie," she said.

I was giggling and waving good-bye when Mom walked in.

All of a sudden, everything changed.

Mom looked at the bunch of my hair in Hannah's hand.

"Hannah!" she said. "What are you doing?"

"Calm down, Mom." It sounded like Hannah knew Mom would yell. "Cassie's not a little girl anymore."

"What!" I could hear Mom breathing

heavily as she pulled at the hair behind my ear. "Apart from doing this without asking, haven't you two heard of hairdressers?"

Hannah shrugged. I didn't say anything. I was surprised Mom was so angry.

Mom was still fussing behind my ear.

"I'm going to clean it up," Hannah said, but her voice sounded unsure now.

"Look how short it is here!" Mom yelled in my ear. "How on earth are you going to clean up this piece?"

Hannah leaned in and started breathing heavily into my ear, too.

Then she said, "How did that piece get so short?"

Now I was worried.

"When you cut hair in a pigtail," Mom said quietly, "you end up with different lengths. All the hair is pulled from different parts of the head, so you end up with some long pieces and some REALLY SHORT PIECES!"

Hannah gasped.

I jumped up and started yelling, too.

"Hannah, what did you do?" I yelled. I suddenly felt scared and angry.

"It's OK," Hannah said, but her voice sounded wobbly. "I can fix it."

As my mind raced, I felt the short hair behind my ear. In some places, it was so short it felt prickly. Why had Hannah cut it like that?

Then I realized what Hannah had done.

"You tricked me!" I yelled. "You did this to me because you hate me looking cute!"

Hannah rolled her eyes. "Yes, I hate you looking cute," she yelled back. "You're nine years old!"

"You did this to me on purpose!"

Now I was crying. Half of my hair was gone, and my big sister had done it to me because she hates me.

"You want me to look ugly!"

"Yeah, right," Hannah yelled. "I'm the EVIL BIG SISTER." She was yelling even louder than Mom or me.

Then Hannah ran to her room and slammed the door.

Mom looked at me and shook her head.

"I'll call the hairdresser," she said.

✽

When we came home from the hairdresser, Hannah was still in her bedroom. My room is next to Hannah's, but I couldn't hear any noise coming from next door.

I looked in the mirror. A stranger with short hair stared back at me. My hair was so short, it looked like it had been shaved in some places. I looked like a different person.

What would Dad think?

He calls me his beautiful little girl, but I didn't feel beautiful or little anymore.

We were going to see Dad and his girlfriend Felicity over the weekend. I wondered how much my hair would grow in three days.

I still felt angry that Hannah had tricked me. She had planned it all along. She was so mean!

I lay down on my bed, feeling bad. My long hair was gone and Hannah hated me more than ever.

Hannah is so mean to me.

✳

CHAPTER THREE

For dinner, we had my favorite food —pizza.

Mom kept saying, "Cheer up, Cassie. You look great!" But she looked tired and sad.

Hannah just stared at her plate. She loves pizza, too, but she only ate one slice. Then she went back to her bedroom.

After dinner, I turned on the TV. I sat in the best chair, even though it was Hannah's turn. I wanted Hannah to walk in and tell me it was her turn in the chair. Then I would yell back at her, and ask her why she had cut my hair so short.

But Hannah didn't come in, so I turned off the TV.

I went to bed and tried to sleep.

I wanted the day to be over. But it was too early to sleep. I lay in the dark, feeling more and more angry.

Then I noticed something.

A tiny crack of light was coming from my closet.

My closet was built into the wall, so it was strange to see light coming from it. Where was the light coming from?

A toy? A flashlight? Maybe it was a magic door.

It was pretty dark in my room, but I could see OK. I crept along the carpet to where my closet meets the wall. Then I slid the door open, and waited.

Nothing happened.

The crack of light was coming from the side of the closet, right in front of me. I leaned in closer, trying to see better. The light seemed to get brighter.

What could the light be?

Suddenly, I understood. It made sense.

The light wasn't coming from inside my closet—it was coming from Hannah's room.

Hannah and I both have closets built into the same wall. Hannah's closet faces into her room and mine faces into my room.

I peered further into my closet. There was a gap between the edge of the closet and the wall. I could just see the gap on Hannah's side, too.

The light was coming from Hannah's room and through her closet. I could see her room through the gaps.

How strange! The builder must have made a mistake and not bothered to fix it.

Then I had an idea.

The gap wasn't very wide, but neither am I. I leaned forward until my head slipped through the gap. Then I turned my shoulders to the side and carefully slid my whole body through.

I was standing between the two closets in the wall. It felt a bit cramped and dusty. I barely had room to move. But it was exciting, like a tiny, secret room.

I squeezed my head through the gap leading to Hannah's closet and peeked out through the hanging clothes.

I felt like a secret spy.

I hadn't found a magic door but I had found something better—a secret door into Hannah's room!

Hannah was sitting on her bed and reading. I could just see part of Hannah's head, but I couldn't see what she was reading.

Hannah just sat there, turning the pages and reading. Nothing was happening, but I didn't feel bored. I felt good, like I had something really secret and useful.

Hannah didn't want to watch TV with

me. She didn't even want to talk to me.
But I could still watch her.

Then Hannah did something.

She picked her nose!

Then she wiped it on her bed. Yuck!

I stayed in the secret spot for a long
time, just watching.

❋

CHAPTER FOUR

The next morning, I was extra slow walking to school. Hannah is supposed to walk with me before she heads off to high school. But today, she walked ahead without even looking at me.

I kicked at stones and shuffled my feet. I thought about telling Mom that Hannah hadn't walked with me to school.

I wanted Hannah to get into trouble

for being so mean. But I knew she would hate me even more if I told Mom.

When I finally made it to school, the bell had just rung.

Perfect timing.

I slipped into the end of the line, hoping no one would notice my hair.

My plan worked for about twenty seconds. That's how long it took to walk into the classroom and sit down.

Bec, who sits next to me, noticed right away.

"Cassie! Oh, look at your hair!" she said sadly. "It's all gone . . . your beautiful hair. . . ."

I didn't know what to say. I just wanted

Bec to stop talking about it. But by now, the whole class was staring at me.

Everyone was looking at me and talking about my hair.

"You cut your hair, Cassie!"

"Look at Cassie!"

I could feel my face turning red.

This is all Hannah's fault.

This was all Hannah's fault.

"Looks like you had a fight with a lawn mower," Adrian said. I don't like Adrian. He has dirty fingernails.

After that, nothing bad really happened. Mrs. Bonacci chose me to be snack monitor.

That was good.

At lunchtime, the girls were all really nice, too. They all said my hair looked good. They tried to make me feel better. Everyone kept touching it and saying how soft it felt.

At the end of the day, even Sam talked to me.

"See you tomorrow, funky girl," he said and smiled.

Wow, Sam noticed me.

I kind of like Sam, but that's a secret.

After school, walking with Mom through the grocery store was different, too. When I had long hair, old ladies would smile at me. Some would even try to talk to me. But none of them did that today. It was like they didn't notice me anymore.

The lady with lots of makeup who works at the deli always used to give me a piece of chicken to eat.

But not today. She didn't even recognize me!

The TV show was right—I really do look different with short hair. But more than that, people think I'm a different sort of person. They don't treat me like a little girl anymore.

I started to feel glad that people weren't treating me like a doll anymore. I didn't have to be the good little girl —I could just be myself.

Now I could start to grow up.

CHAPTER FIVE

When we got home from shopping, I was still feeling bad about Hannah. She was at band practice, so while Mom was putting the groceries away, I sneaked into Hannah's room. I wanted to see what she had been reading last night.

Hannah's room is always really messy. She has clothes all over the floor, and books and magazines all over her desk.

But she has some good pictures on her wall. There's even a picture of Orlando Towner. Hannah says he's the most gorgeous guy in the world, but I'm not sure what's so good about him.

There was only a clock radio on Hannah's bedside table. I searched around her desk and bookshelf. But none of the books there looked like the one that Hannah had been reading last night.

Then I looked under Hannah's bed.

There it was—the book from last night. Hannah had slipped it under her bed as though she didn't want Mom to know what she was reading.

I pulled the book out.

The cover said *Ghosts and Spirits—Real-Life Sightings*. There was a picture of an old-fashioned room with big windows and a fuzzy white splotch in the middle. I stared at the splotch, but it didn't look like a ghost to me.

I flicked through the book. It showed lots of splotches. I read about someone who used to hear ghosts walking down the hall.

Suddenly, I heard something.

I held my breath and listened.

There it was again. Voices.

Ghost voices?

No. Hannah must have come home and was talking to Mom in the kitchen.

I slipped the ghost book back under Hannah's bed and tiptoed to her door.

I was just about to sneak out when I heard the hall door open.

Oh, no! Hannah would see me if I opened her door now.

I was trapped in her room!

I stumbled back from Hannah's bedroom door, almost tripping on a pair of jeans. She was about to catch me sneaking around in her room.

Then I remembered my secret place.

There was a gap in the side of Hannah's closet, too. That's how I could see into her room last night.

I could hear Hannah walking down the hall. Quickly, I squeezed into Hannah's closet. I stepped on something that snapped under one foot, and crushed a box under the other, but I had no time to be careful.

I slipped into the secret space in the wall just as Hannah opened her door.

**Phew ...
just in time.**

I held my breath and froze. If I could see through the gap, then Hannah could, too—if she looked carefully.

I pressed my back into the wall, trying to be as small and quiet as possible.

I couldn't see Hannah now, but I could hear some clothes rustling as though she was taking off her school uniform.

Would she come and look in the closet to choose some clothes?

I saw a flicker of dark hair as Hannah leaned down to pick up some jeans from the floor. I was lucky she was so messy.

I breathed as quietly as I could.

Hannah pulled something out of her bag. I realized she had no idea that I was there, hiding. Watching her.

This was amazing. I had already found out about the ghost book. What else could I learn about Hannah?

I felt as though the ghost book was important, but I couldn't think why.

I needed to watch Hannah some more.

CHAPTER SIX

At dinner, I told Mom about being snack monitor. I felt happy, and Mom seemed happy, too. Hannah just looked down at her fried rice without smiling.

"How was band practice?" I asked Hannah.

She glanced over at me. For a moment, I thought she wasn't going to answer at all. Then she looked back down at her rice.

"Fine," she said.

Mom sighed. She started looking sad again. I felt angry that Hannah could make us all feel bad.

"Pass the soy sauce, please," I said. I didn't really want any soy sauce, but it was right in front of Hannah. I wanted to see what she would do.

Hannah just kept eating.

Rude, huh?

Being ignored by Hannah was almost worse than when she cut my hair.

Mom shook her head and reached over to give me the soy sauce.

"Hannah's been chosen for the band concert," Mom said. "She's done really well."

Hannah would be really pleased with

that. She loves playing the flute. But she kept on staring at her rice and eating.

Mom sighed again.

Normally, I would have been happy for Hannah. But now things were different. I wasn't cute anymore, and I didn't want to be nice.

So I just shrugged and stared down at my rice like Hannah.

I couldn't see poor Mom because I was staring at my rice, but I could tell she wasn't smiling.

After dinner, Hannah went straight to her room. I was about to do the same when the phone rang.

It was Dad. He talked happily about our visit over the weekend. He was planning on taking us for a dim sum lunch, then to the park.

Dad asked how I was doing.

"Good," I said. "I was snack monitor today."

But I couldn't tell him about my hair.

Over the phone, Dad still thought I was his beautiful little girl. In some ways, that was nice.

"And I have a surprise, too," I said.

"Surprise, huh?" Dad said. "Sounds interesting."

I could still be Dad's little girl for a few more days. *Then* he would see the surprise.

While Hannah was talking to Dad, I went to my room. It was dark now, but

I didn't turn the light on. Feeling like a spy, I slipped into my secret spot. Ready.

When Hannah went back to her room, she lay on her tummy on the bed and pulled out the ghost book. She loves that book.

Hmmmmm . . . ghosts.

I watched Hannah's legs on the bed and wondered why she read that book so much. Did she really think those white splotches in the pictures were ghosts?

Did Hannah believe ghosts were real?

As I watched Hannah from my secret spot, an idea came to me. I smiled to myself. It was the perfect way to find out if Hannah believed in ghosts. I waited for a while, watching Hannah. Then I did it.

Scratch, scratch, scratch.

I felt a bit silly, scratching the wall, but it was part of my new plan. Maybe Hannah would think I was a ghost in the wall. I wanted to see what she would do.

Scratch, scratch, scratch.

I waited. But Hannah kept reading. This was boring.

I tried one more time.

Scratch, scratch, scratch.

Suddenly, Hannah moved. She sat up on the bed, facing the closet.

I held my breath and did it one last time.

Scratch, scratch, scratch.

But Hannah just shrugged. She rolled over and kept on reading.

Maybe Hannah didn't believe in ghosts after all.

❁

CHAPTER *SEVEN*

The next morning at breakfast, Hannah said, "I think there's a mouse in my closet."

I hid a smile.

"What!" said Mom. Mom's a neat freak, and really doesn't like mice. "Is there some food hidden under all that mess?" she asked Hannah.

"I don't think so." Hannah frowned down at her cornflakes.

"Well, let's have a cleanup," Mom said and rubbed her hands together. She liked the idea of cleaning Hannah's room.

"I'll do it tonight," Hannah said quickly. "OK? Don't go in my room."

Mom looked disappointed. "OK," she said sadly.

After school, Hannah started cleaning up her room. I didn't have to hide in the secret spot to know what Hannah was doing. I could hear her throwing things in the closet. Clean room, messy closet—that was Hannah.

While Hannah was cleaning, I went through my box of hair ties and clips. I put all the hair ties in a bag and put them in a drawer. It would be a long time before I could use them again.

My hair was almost too short even for the clips. I tried putting two in my hair. Maybe I could wear them tomorrow to see Dad. But they looked a bit silly. They suited a little girl with long hair.

After a while, I put all the clips away with the hair ties.

Then I looked around my room. It was totally different from Hannah's. There was a pile of teddy bears and dolls in one corner. Another corner had an old wooden stove that I used to play with. There was even a Bananas in Pajamas growth chart on the wall.

It looked like a baby's room.

I pulled down the Bananas in Pajamas chart and stared at the blank space on the wall. What should I put there instead? I didn't like Orlando Towner.

Who did I like?

After a while, I listened for Hannah.

I couldn't hear her throwing things in the closet anymore. Everything was quiet.

I turned out the light in my room and slid quietly into the secret spot. It was extra dark because Hannah's closet door was shut properly.

As my eyes got used to the darkness, I could see all the clothes and junk Hannah had thrown in the closet. There was even a bag and some clothes blocking the gap leading to Hannah's closet.

I smiled in the darkness. Hannah had cleaned up her room because of my scratching. That felt good—she couldn't ignore me completely.

What could I do next?

CHAPTER EIGHT

I stood in the darkness in my secret spot, thinking about ghosts again. If mice scratch, what noise do ghosts make?

They stomp around at night.

I couldn't see into Hannah's room, but that was OK. If her closet door was shut, then I was completely hidden, too.

I reached into her closet and thumped on the door.

Thump, thump, thump, thump.

Ha! Mice didn't thump. I waited, but nothing happened. Maybe Hannah wasn't in her room.

I tried again.

Thump, thump, thump, thump.

Still nothing.

Suddenly, Hannah's closet door slid open. A shoe and a CD stand toppled out onto Hannah's feet.

I blinked in the sudden light and leaned back into the shadows. Had Hannah seen me? I pushed my back into the wall behind me.

Everything was quiet.

I saw Hannah lift her arm to scratch her head. Then she leaned down to pick up the shoe and CD stand. She jammed them back into the closet and lay back down on the bed.

That had been close, but the hiding place had worked. Hannah hadn't seen me. She would never notice the gap if

I kept the light out in my room.

I leaned forward and peeked into Hannah's room. I could see her legs on the bed. She was on her tummy, facing the other way.

Hannah had left her closet door open, so now I couldn't reach it. It was open too far.

Instead, I reached down to touch the CD stand. It was lying down, folded shut. That was good. I didn't want the noise to come right from my hiding spot.

I couldn't lift the CD stand, but I gave it a wiggle and a shove. It rattled against the wooden floor.

Rattle, rattle, clang.

Right away, Hannah jumped back up. I couldn't see her, but I could hear her breathing now.

She stood in front of the closet for a while, and then she started pulling all her stuff out. Everything that had gone in came out again, plus all the things that were in there to start with.

She wasn't quiet about it, either. As Hannah pulled and rattled and threw, I slipped quietly out of the hiding space, back into my room.

Easy.

It seemed very tidy and peaceful in my room.

I switched on my reading lamp and

pretended to read as I listened to Hannah empty her closet.

She was making a lot of noise. Mom must have heard it, too.

"Hannah!" Mom didn't sound pleased. "What are you doing?"

I couldn't hear Hannah reply.

"You're supposed to be cleaning up this mess."

"Mom," Hannah was speaking softly. "There's something. . . ."

"What? A mouse?" Mom still sounded annoyed. "Clean up this mess and I'll set a mouse trap tomorrow."

Hannah stayed quiet. I knew she didn't

think the thumping and rattling had come from a mouse.

I couldn't stop grinning. This was great fun. Plus, Hannah deserved it.

"That's for the bad haircut, Hannah," I whispered to myself.

CHAPTER NINE

The next day was Saturday—the start of our weekend with Dad.

When I climbed out of bed, I suddenly felt nervous. What would Dad say when he saw my hair? What would Felicity say?

I bit my lip, staring into my closet and trying to decide what to wear. Finally, I decided not to worry. I put on my favorite pair of black jeans and a purple

T-shirt that said "Hey, Girl!" on the front. At least I would be comfortable.

When Dad and Felicity arrived, Hannah was in front of me. Dad hugged her first.

"Hey, Cassie girl!" Felicity said and patted my hair. "Look at you!"

By then, Dad had seen me.

"Cassie!" Dad said, and gave me a hug. "My beautiful little girl," he said. But he was frowning over my head at Mom.

"Surprise!" I said meekly. My face was burning.

"Why did you let her do that?" Dad asked Mom angrily.

Mom shrugged. "Ask the girls," she said, half smiling.

Dad looked at me. I gulped.

Dad looked around like he was deciding who to yell at.

But before he could say anything, Felicity said, "Let's go. I'm hungry."

Thank goodness for Felicity.

Felicity talked the whole way in the

car about how she had shaved her head when she was eighteen. I tried to imagine what Felicity would have looked like, but it was pretty hard. These days, she has fluffy brown hair that floats around her shoulders.

I could see Dad frowning while Felicity talked. He hated my hair. But I didn't feel sad like I thought I would. I felt annoyed. Why did I have to look like Dad wanted me to? Why couldn't I have really short hair if I wanted? Short hair didn't hurt anyone.

Hannah was scowling out the window, just like Dad.

I could see where she got it from.

When we sat down for dim sum, Felicity was still talking and Dad was still frowning.

I had just managed to choose a plate of pork dumplings from the cart when Dad finally said something.

"Did your mother let you cut your hair like that, Cassie?" Dad said. He said it like Mom had let me jump off a cliff.

I glanced at Hannah and bit into the soft dumpling. She looked white.

"Nope," I said, with my mouth full. Then I swallowed. "The hairdresser said it would suit me." That was true in a way.

"The hairdresser!" Dad looked around like he wanted to go and yell at the hairdresser.

Hannah was watching me with her mouth open. She still looked pale.

"But you're only nine years old!" Dad said, a little too loudly for a restaurant.

"So?" I yelled back. "I'm not a little girl anymore, Dad." I had heard those words somewhere before, but I couldn't think where.

I'm not
a little girl!

Hannah was watching me closely now, half smiling.

Dad was turning red. But he didn't know what to say. My hair was already short, so what could he do? He took a gulp of tea.

Felicity saved the day. "Go, Cassie!" she said. "Fight for your rights, girl."

I like Felicity.

❁

CHAPTER TEN

On Sunday night, we were back home and I was back in my secret hiding place.

Hannah was at her desk doing homework. I couldn't see her, but I could hear her turning pages.

I felt really good. I didn't care what people thought of my hair anymore. And I wasn't scared of Hannah. Short hair made me feel like a different person.

I picked up an old sneaker from the bottom of Hannah's closet and threw it into Hannah's room. I couldn't throw very well because I could only move my wrist, but I heard it thump on the carpet.

Right away, I heard Hannah gasp.

I leaned back into the wall, but I couldn't hear anything.

Then I heard Hannah stand up. I could hear her breathing quickly, as she crouched on the end of her bed, facing the closet.

I thought quickly. This was it. Time for the real fun.

I moved my feet to get balanced, then I thumped my hip against the side of Hannah's closet.

Thud.

Hannah gasped again and crawled backwards to the top of her bed.

I did it again.

Thud.

Then, I let out a growl from the back of my throat, "Grrrrrrruuuugh. . . ."

I saw the bed move as Hannah climbed off. I couldn't see her now, but I heard her bedroom door open.

Where was she going?

Suddenly, the light turned on in my bedroom. Hannah was checking my room! Clever Hannah.

I pushed back into the wall, trying to be as small as possible. The gap into my bedroom was right near my shoulder and my closet door was open. She would notice me for sure.

I couldn't see Hannah, but I could hear her breathing as she looked in my closet.

I stayed very still.

This was it.

Hannah was about to catch me.

I waited for Hannah to say something. But she didn't. Instead, she turned out my bedroom light, and was gone. I heard the hall door open and then shut.

I breathed out and leaned against the wall. I couldn't believe Hannah hadn't seen my shoulder through the gap.

I slipped out of the hiding spot and spent a few minutes in the bathroom. Then I went to find Hannah.

She was sitting in the living room. She was very still. Her face was white and her eyes were big. Then she saw me.

"Where have you been?" Hannah asked, but she sounded glad to see me.

"In the bathroom," I said. I wasn't sure if she'd believe me, but I switched on the TV and sat in the best chair.

Hannah nodded and tried to smile.

"Shouldn't you be doing your homework?" I said. I tried to sound normal, but I wasn't used to talking to Hannah anymore.

Hannah nodded again.

"I think I'll do it out here," she said. But she didn't go and get her homework. She didn't move.

I pretended to watch TV, but my mind was racing. Hannah looked really scared. She had even forgotten not to talk to me.

I sat there, feeling a bit bad. I hadn't meant to scare Hannah this much. I just wanted to annoy her. I always thought she would figure out it was me. I just wanted

her to stop ignoring me. That was all.
Suddenly, it had all gone too far.

What have
I done?

✿

CHAPTER ELEVEN

The next morning, Hannah's face was pale and there were dark patches under her eyes. She didn't look like she had slept very well.

When we were leaving for school, Hannah said, "Cassie, do you ever hear things in your closet?"

"Like what?" I said. I didn't know what else to say.

"Like, um, banging?" Hannah looked at me sideways.

I shrugged, but I felt bad. Should I tell Hannah it was me? I didn't want her to stop talking to me again.

"No," I said, feeling guilty.

Hannah frowned down at her feet as she walked.

"It's probably nothing," I said hopefully.

That was it. I decided to stop knocking in the closet. No more games. Then Hannah would stop being scared. And if she never knew it was me in the wall, she would keep talking to me.

Perfect.

But the next morning, Hannah looked even worse. I had stopped banging, but Hannah was still scared.

At breakfast on the third morning, Hannah was so tired she looked sick.

Mom kept frowning as she watched Hannah. But Hannah was too tired to notice us watching her. She buttered a piece of toast and tried to cut it with her knife upside down. Hannah looked down at her knife as though she didn't understand why it wasn't cutting.

"Hannah, are you OK?" Mom said.

Hannah nodded and picked up her whole piece of toast to eat.

"Maybe you should stay home today,"

Mom said. "Get some rest in bed."

"Bed? No." Hannah looked scared. "I'm OK, Mom."

She put down the toast after one bite.

On the way to school, I felt like I had to look after Hannah rather than the other way around. I steered her around some dog poo on the sidewalk. She would have stepped in it for sure. I checked for cars as we crossed the road.

When we made it to my school, I watched Hannah walk slowly towards the high school. When would Hannah stop feeling frightened?

I had stopped banging days ago. Why was she still scared?

That night, I lay in bed worrying about Hannah. It was late, but Hannah had only just gone to bed.

I wished I could help Hannah without making her angry with me.

After a while, I climbed out of bed and slid into my secret spot. I wanted to check on Hannah.

It was completely dark and quiet. I listened carefully. Was Hannah asleep?

I could just barely hear Hannah sobbing in her bed. She wasn't sleeping, she was crying!

This is horrible!

I had to tell Hannah the truth.

Even if she stopped talking to me again, I had to tell her. Anything was better than this.

I slipped out of the secret spot and went to Hannah's bedroom door. But I didn't knock. I didn't want to scare her even more.

"Hannah," I said. "Are you awake?"

I heard her sniffing and sitting up in bed, but she didn't turn on the light.

"Are you OK?" I asked as I walked into Hannah's room.

Suddenly, Hannah started crying hard.

"I'm so scared," she said between sobs.

I reached over and hugged her. But now Hannah was crying harder—deep, painful sobs that shook her whole body.

"It's OK, Hannah," I said. "Don't be scared." I curled her hair behind her ears.

"There's nothing to be scared of," I said. But Hannah kept sobbing as though she hadn't heard me. I had to calm her down.

"Come into my room," I said. "You can sleep with me in my bed."

That helped.

"OK," said Hannah between sobs. "But don't tell Mom."

"OK," I whispered. I picked up Hannah's pillow and took her hand. I led her into my bedroom.

Once I told Hannah what I'd done, she wouldn't talk to me for a very long time.

CHAPTER TWELVE

I put Hannah's pillow on the end of my bed and we both snuggled in with our heads on the two ends. I'm so short that there was still a lot of room.

Hannah had stopped crying now. She rested her legs against mine, as though she was glad to be touching someone. It felt good.

"Hannah," I said quietly. This was going to be hard.

But I didn't get a chance to say anything.

"I'm sorry I cut your hair," Hannah said in the dark. Her voice sounded clear and calm.

"That's OK," I said quietly. But I still didn't understand. "Why did you do it, Hannah?" I asked.

"I didn't mean to," Hannah said. "It was an accident. I didn't think about what would happen when I cut off your pigtail."

I was stunned. "You mean it really was an accident?" I said.

"Yeah. Sorry."

My mind raced. Hannah has always

been bigger than me, better than me, smarter than me. I never even imagined that she made mistakes.

"You mean, you didn't plan to cut it like that?" I said.

"Nope." Hannah sounded like she was smiling. "But it looks OK, don't you think?"

"But why did you stop talking to me?" I said. "If it was a mistake, why did you blame me?"

"Blame you? You blamed me!" Hannah said. "Did *you* know what would happen if I cut off a pigtail?"

I didn't say anything. I'd had no idea.

"You didn't know either, did you?"

Hannah said. "We didn't realize how short some pieces would be."

Hannah moved her legs away from mine.

"But I'm the one who got yelled at. Just because I'm older, I'm not allowed to make a mistake."

I stayed quiet, thinking.

"And then you started crying and yelling," Hannah went on. "You just acted like a baby again, and Mom felt sorry for you. I hate that."

Was it my fault, too? Was I blaming Hannah all this time, when it was partly my fault, too?

We were both quiet. I thought about the day Hannah had cut my hair. It seemed

like a long time ago—when I still felt like
a little girl.

Hannah moved her legs back to touch
mine. She didn't seem angry anymore.

"Why didn't you tell Dad what
happened?" Hannah asked quietly.

I sighed. "I don't know," I said. "It has

nothing to do with Dad. It's between you and me."

"He was so angry!" Hannah giggled.

I giggled, too.

Now it all seemed really silly.

"Yeah, thank goodness for Felicity," I said.

That did it. Now we were really laughing.

"THANK GOODNESS for Felicity!" Hannah repeated in a funny voice, trying not to laugh too hard.

After that, we giggled and talked and tried to stay quiet until we fell asleep.

It turned out to be a really good night.

✿

CHAPTER THIRTEEN

For the next few nights, Hannah sneaked into bed with me. She stopped looking so scared and she started sleeping well. She started talking to me again, too.

Hannah even helped me fix up my room. She offered me a poster of Orlando Towner to put up on the wall, but I said no thanks. I don't like Orlando Towner.

In the end, I put up a poster of Kayla

Storm. Maybe I'll try to grow my hair to look like her, too.

Hannah helped me pack away all the teddy bears and dolls. She was about to throw them in my closet, but I told her that a messy closet was bad luck.

Hannah looked at me strangely when I said that.

I never told Hannah about the secret spot or what I'd done. It doesn't seem to matter anymore. And Hannah never told me that she believes in ghosts. But we talk about lots of other things.

These days, Hannah still sneaks into my bed some nights. But I don't think she's scared anymore. I think she sleeps in my bed when she wants to talk.

Hannah told me about Josh, who plays the clarinet in the school band. And I told her about Sam, even though there's not much to tell.

Hannah doesn't hate me anymore. I'm not sure exactly when she changed her mind. Maybe it was me that changed. I don't just mean my hair—these days I never feel like a little girl, I just feel like me.

THE END

Go GiRL! #4

Lunchtime Rules

BY
VICKI STEGGALL

If this lunchtime doesn't end soon, I'm going to explode. It's gone on forever and ever and I'm sick of it. I'm sure the bell should have rung ages ago.

It's been another horrible, endless lunchtime. Just like all the others since everything went wrong and my friends started playing without me.

I can hear them, just over there

behind me, playing soccer. My favorite. My best friend Ellie is shouting our cheer song. That's what we always shouted when we won against the boys.

It's just so unfair! Hearing Ellie makes my eyes sting. I stare into my lunch box, which looks all blurry. The girls I'm sitting with haven't noticed yet—they're busy talking. I really don't want to start crying in front of them, so I blink my eyes hard and try to stop my breath from coming out in little shudders. . . .

Karen, sitting next to me, looks over. "Are you OK?" she asks. Karen is kind to everyone.

I nod my head, but my breathing has

started to come in gasps and everything's gone blurry again.

"It must be awful not playing," she says gently. "You're so good at all those games, even though you're small."

I nod, but don't look up from my lunch box. I don't want to talk about it, even to Karen.

It *is* awful—and being small is exactly what started it all. Now I hate lunchtime and I hate school. And I hate sitting here having to hear them playing. . . .

I just want everything to go back to the way it was.

But what's the chance of that ever happening?